COUCH
POTATOES!

by MORT WALKER and DIK BROWNE

TOR

A TOM DOHERTY ASSOCIATES BOOK
NEW YORK

HI & LOIS: COUCH POTATOES

A TOR Book
Published by Tom Doherty Associates, Inc.
49 West 24 Street
New York, NY 10010

ISBN: 0-812-50603-0   Can. ISBN: 0-812-50604-9

First edition: January 1990

Printed in the United States of America

0 9 8 7 6 5 4 3 2 1

"THEY ALWAYS GO STRAIGHT ACROSS... THEY NEVER GO WIBBLY, WOBBLY..."

WHO COMES HOME TIRED AT NIGHT, BUT STILL HELPS MOM WITH THE DISHES, READS US STORIES, GOES TO PTA OR WORKS ON CHECKBOOKS?

ON HIS DAYS "OFF," WHO CUTS THE LAWN, CLEANS THE BASEMENT, FIXES THE ROOF, PAINTS THE BEDROOM AND WAXES THE KITCHEN FLOOR?

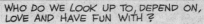

WHO DO WE LOOK UP TO, DEPEND ON, LOVE AND HAVE FUN WITH?

SUPER DADDY!!

HE JUST CAME UP AND PUT THESE IN MY LAP

COOKIES

DIK BROWNE

6-16 © King Features Syndicate, Inc., 1974. World rights reserved.

DIK BROWNE —

PLEASE DISTURB

1-20

DIK BROWNE —

I'VE JUST DECIDED, PLAYING "FOLLOW THE LEADER" WITH DAWG ISN'T ALL THAT MUCH FUN!

4-28

2-15

WELL, LET'S SEE...WHEN YOU WERE ONLY A YEAR OLD, I USED TO BUNDLE YOU UP IN YOUR SNOWSUIT AND TAKE YOU IN THE STROLLER SHOPPING WITH ME...

WE USED TO LOOK IN THE SHOP WINDOWS, YOU LIKED TO WAVE AT THE POLICEMAN ON THE CORNER, I USED TO BUY YOU A LOLLIPOP AT BISSELL'S DRUGSTORE...

DITTO FLAGSTONE, YOU HAVE YOUR THUMB IN YOUR MOUTH.

MMM

I ALWAYS SUCK MY THUMB WHEN I GO BACK TO THE OLD DAYS!

2-8

DIK BROWNE

HEY, MOM! CAN YOU COME UP FROM THE BASEMENT FOR A MINUTE?

WHAT'S WRONG?

NOTHING! I JUST BET DOT I COULD GO THROUGH THE KITCHEN WITHOUT TOUCHING THE FLOOR!

4-18

DIK BROWNE

5-9

5-16

BEETLE BAILEY

THE WACKIEST G.I. IN THE ARMY

☐ 56126-0	BEETLE BAILEY: WELCOME TO CAMP SWAMPY!	$3.95
☐ 56127-9		Canada $4.95
☐ 56109-0	BEETLE BAILEY: THIN AIR	$2.95
☐ 56111-2	BEETLE BAILEY: THREE'S A CROWD	$2.95
☐ 56068-X	BEETLE BAILEY #4: NOT REVERSE	$1.95
☐ 56128-7	BEETLE BAILEY: SEPARATE CHECKS	$3.95
☐ 56129-5		Canada $4.95
☐ 56092-2	BEETLE BAILEY #8: SURPRISE PACKAGE	$2.50
☐ 56093-0		Canada $2.95
☐ 56124-4	BEETLE BAILEY: THAT SINKING FEELING	$1.95
☐ 56125-2		Canada $2.50